Dora's
Super Silly Coloring Book

A GOLDEN BOOK • NEW YORK

The works in this collection were originally published separately and in slightly different form by Golden Books as *Super Friends!*, illustrated by Jason Fruchter, in 2004; *Pony Express*, illustrated by Piero Piluso, in 2002; *The Circus Lion/Bouncy Ball*, illustrated by Bob Roper and Susan Hall, in 2003; *It's Fiesta Time!*, illustrated by Piero Piluso, in 2004; and *Monster Bash!*, illustrated by Susan Hall, in 2004.
ISBN: 978-0-375-87308-9
www.randomhouse.com/kids
Printed in the United States of America
10 9 8 7 6 5 4 3

¡Hola! I'm Dora!
Today is Best Friends Day!

My best friend is furry and has a long tail.
What's that monkey's name? It's Boots!

I'm meeting Boots for a Best Friends Day picnic, and
I'm bringing him sweet, yummy strawberries as a surprise!
Will you help me find 10 strawberries to bring to Boots?

Boots and I are going to meet each other on top
of Rainbow Rock! But how do we get there?
Let's stop and think.

Who do we ask when we don't know the way to go?
Right! We ask Map!

Map says we have to go through the Gate to get to Rainbow Rock.

Will you help me find the Gate?
Trace the path that leads to it so I know the way to go.

Hi, I'm Boots! I can't wait to meet Dora at
Rainbow Rock for the Best Friends Day picnic!
I'm bringing chocolate as a special surprise!

© Viacom International Inc.

**Happy Best Friends Day, Chocolate Tree!
Do you have any chocolate I can bring to Dora?**

Will you help me get the chocolate?
Draw lines from the chocolate pieces to my bowl.

Now we have to mix the chocolate.
¡Bate, bate, el chocolate!

Mmm, the chocolate is delicious! Dora will love it!
I can't wait to get to Rainbow Rock and give it to her!

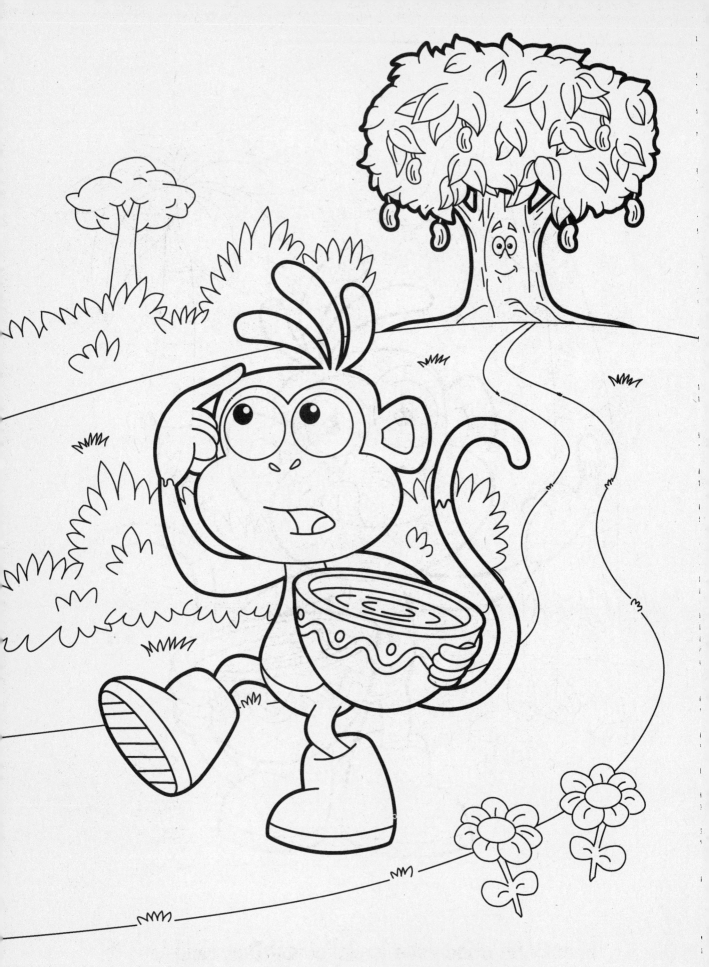

But how will I get to Rainbow Rock?

Map says we need to go past the
Crabby Crabs to get to Rainbow Rock.

Do you see the crabs?
How many Crabby Crabs do you see?

I can't wait to see my best friend, Boots. Hey, look!
There are lots of friends all around.
Circle all the friends.

Benny and Tico are friends who like to share.
Connect the dots to see what they are sharing.

Is Dora on her way to Rainbow Rock?
Great! I love doing things with my best friend!

**Baby Blue Bird has a best friend.
It's Big Red Chicken!**

Baby Blue Bird and his best friend like to swing.
Happy Best Friends Day!

Oh, no! The Gate is locked, and I have to get through to meet Boots at Rainbow Rock!

I need to use a key to open the lock on the Gate.
Do you see the key?

**What's that? You see Swiper?
Oh, no! He'll try to swipe the key!**

Swiper, no . . . . Oh! Swiper swiped the key.

Will you help find the key?

Thanks for helping Lock find his best friend, Key.

I hear stars. Do you see stars?

Draw lines to connect the stars that look alike.

Which path goes all the way to Rainbow Rock?

There's Rainbow Rock! Thanks for helping!

Oh, no! Map says that Boots needs help
getting past those Crabby Crabs.

How am I going to get past these Crabs?

**Connect the dots to help Boots
swing over the Crabs.**

Wheeeee!

I need to get to Rainbow Rock quickly!
Where's the shortest path to Rainbow Rock?

Yay! I made it to Rainbow Rock!

How am I going to get to the top of
Rainbow Rock to meet Boots?

Will you check Backpack for a rope?

Oh, no! Swiper will try to swipe the rope.

Swiper, no swiping. Swiper, no swiping. Swiper, no swiping!

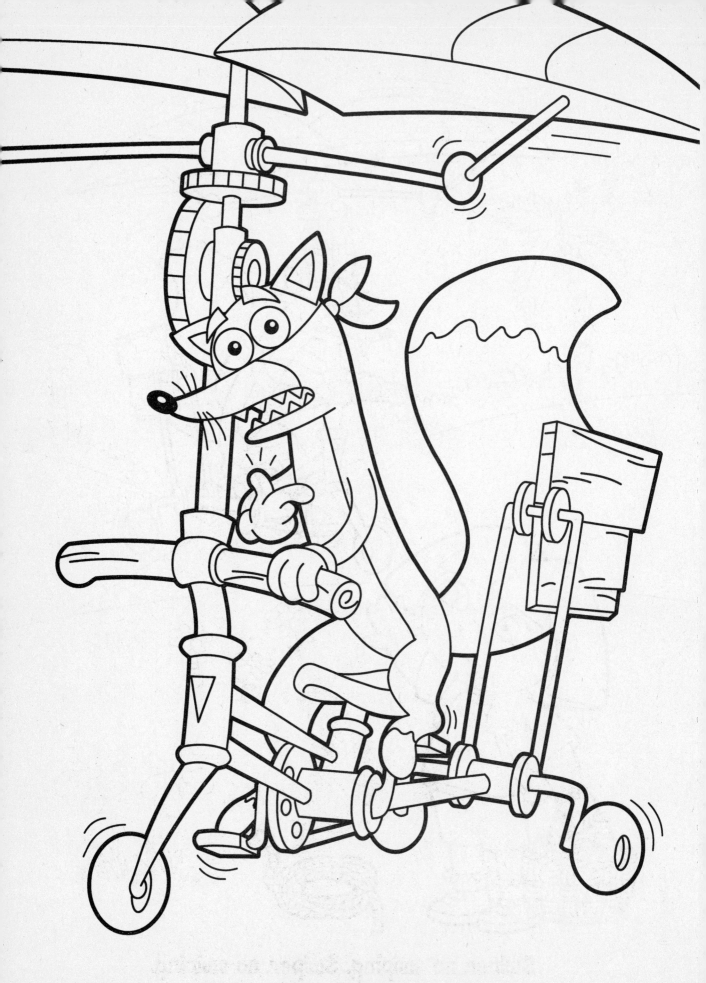

"Oh, mannn!"

Yay! We stopped Swiper.
Now we can go to the picnic.

We made it! Look what I brought, Boots!
Yummy strawberries!

Look what I brought—chocolate!

Happy Best Friends Day, Boots!

Happy Best Friends Day, Dora!

This is the best Best Friends Day ever!

Pony Express!

This is our new friend, Pinto the Pony.

Pinto is going to help us deliver a special package of
Cowboy Cookies. The package has a big star on it.
Do you see the package?

Connect the dots to see who else loves Cowboy Cookies.

We have to deliver the cookies to Benny the Bull.

How will we get to Benny's Barn? We'll have to go through the Gold Mine and through Rattlesnake Rocks to get to Benny's Barn.

Trace the path that will take us to the Gold Mine.

Swiper will try to swipe our cookies. Do you see Swiper?
We have to say, "Swiper, no swiping!"

We made it to the Gold Mine!

We need something to light our way through the Gold Mine. Will you check my backpack to find something we can use?

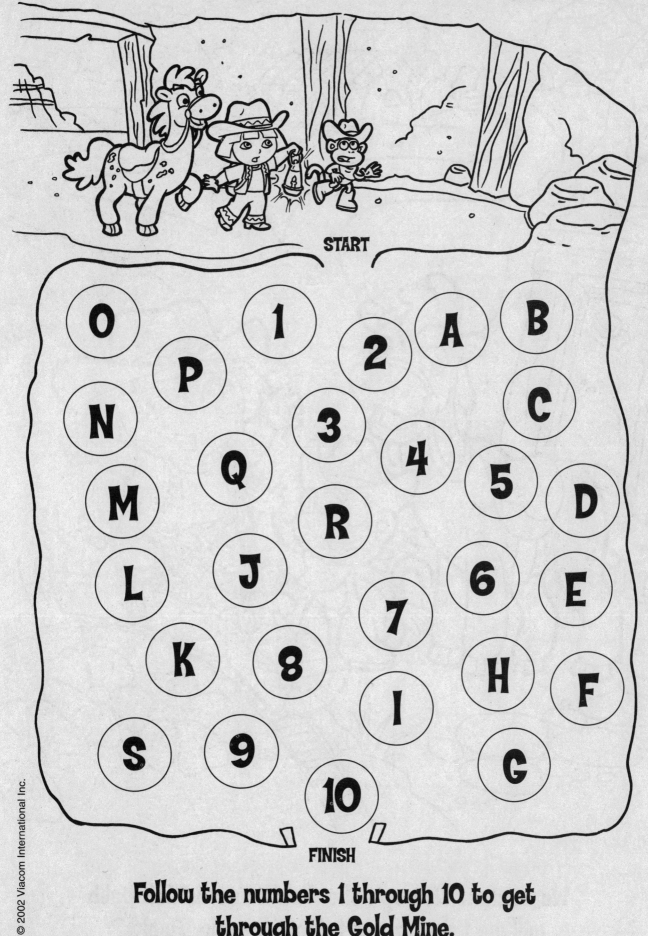

START

O · 1 · 2 · A · B

P · C

N · 3 · 4 · 5 · D

Q · R · 6 · E

M · J

L · 7 · H · F

K · 8 · I · G

S · 9

10

FINISH

Follow the numbers 1 through 10 to get
through the Gold Mine.

We made it through the Gold Mine! Which path
will we take to get to Rattlesnake Rocks?

One cactus is different than the others.
Which one is different?

It's that sneaky fox! We have to say, "Swiper, no swiping!"
so Swiper won't swipe our cookies.

Giddyap, Pinto! Let's take these cookies to Benny!

Stop, Pinto! Oh, no! The cookies are going over the cliff!

We'll lasso those cookies!
Whose rope reached the bag of cookies?

We've reached Rattlesnake Rocks.
Can you find five rattlesnakes?

Yay! We made it past Rattlesnake Rocks! Now we have to take the path with eight rectangles to get to Benny's Barn. Which path has eight rectangles?

We made it to Benny's Barn. Do you see Benny?

Benny is sharing his Cowboy Cookies with everyone! Yummy!

There's one cookie left! Let's give it to Swiper!
Do you see Swiper?

Swiper really loves his Cowboy Cookie!

YEE-HAW! WE DID IT!

Hi! I'm Dora. Boots is waiting for a special package
to arrive in the mail.

Help the mail truck get to Boots's mailbox.

Boots's package has a fire truck inside.
Do you see the box with a fire truck on it?

Oh, no! The fire truck must have fallen
out of the hole in the box.

We have to find the fire truck!

The fire truck is on top of Snowy Mountain.
We'll have to get across Crocodile Lake and through the
tunnel to reach Snowy Mountain.

We have to get to Snowy Mountain before Swiper.
Do you see Swiper?

Oh, no! Swiper heard everything! If he gets to
Snowy Mountain first, he'll swipe the fire truck!

Trace the path that goes to Crocodile Lake.

Connect the dots to find out what will take us to Crocodile Lake really fast!

Let's go, Tico. ¡Vámonos!

We have to stop for the traffic light.

Swiper swiped our steering wheel!

Can you find the steering wheel?

What can we use to get across Crocodile Lake?

We need life jackets so we can be safe.
Backpack has two life jackets! Circle them!

FINISH

START

Help us get through Crocodile Lake.
Watch out for crocodiles!

We made it across Crocodile Lake.
But here comes Swiper!

The train is missing some wheels. Figure out the pattern, and then draw in the missing wheels.

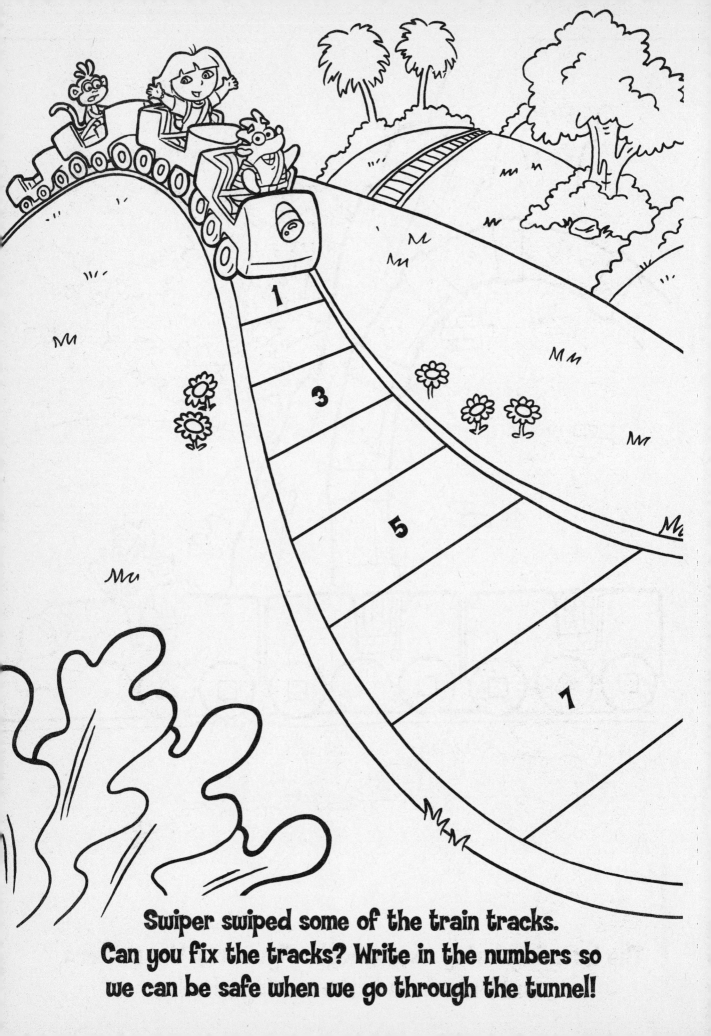

Swiper swiped some of the train tracks.
Can you fix the tracks? Write in the numbers so
we can be safe when we go through the tunnel!

Yay! We made it through the tunnel. Here comes Swiper!
How will Swiper get to the top of the mountain?

Yea! We got past Swiper!

We have to get to the fire truck before Swiper does.
Do you see Swiper? Say, "Swiper, no swiping!"

Yay! We stopped Swiper and got Boots's fire truck!
WE DID IT!

The Circus Lion

Do you like the circus?

Boots is pretending to swing on a trapeze!

Look, Boots! Do you see the circus train?

There it is! Uh-oh, some wheels came off the train.
Draw in the missing wheels to fix the train.

BIG-TOP CIRCUS

There are elephants on the circus train!
How many do you see?

Help the musicians find their instruments.
Match the instrument to its shape.

We want to see a circus lion. Do you see one?

A lion!

This is León, and he wants to join the circus!

Boots is doing a trick.
We want León to show us a circus trick!

That's a great trick! How many balls is León juggling?

Now León is going to juggle with hot dogs!
Will you help him find 6 hot dogs?

Way to go, León!

We have to help León get to the Circus
so he can be a circus lion.
Let's check Map.

We'll have to go through the Swinging Forest, then across Tightrope Bridge. That's how we get to the Circus!

Boy, that Swinging Forest is really far away!

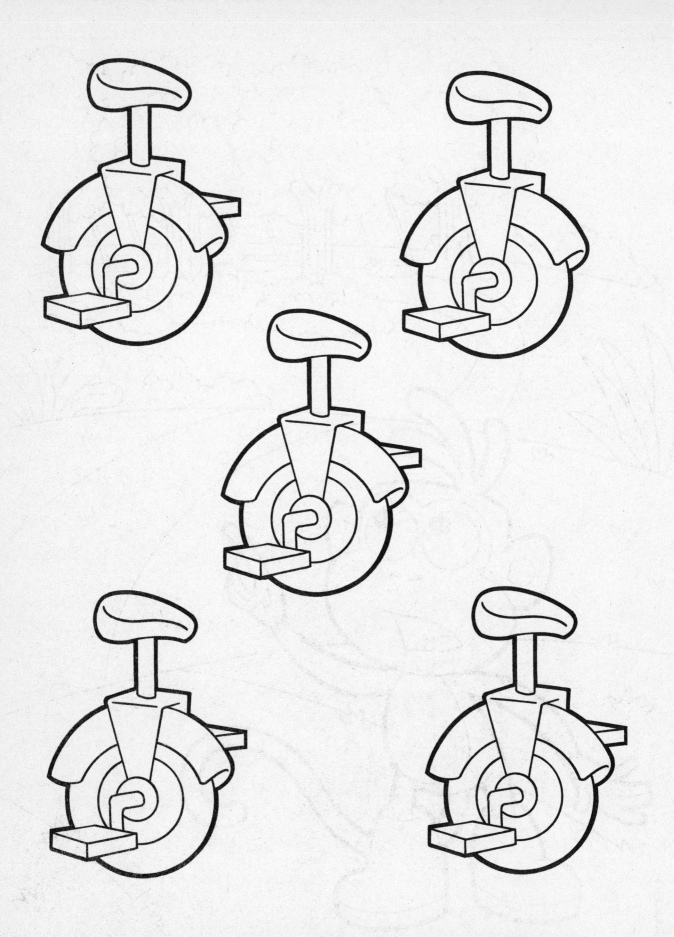

We'll ride León's unicycle to the Swinging Forest.
Do you see the unicycle that's different?

León's unicycle will get us to
the Swinging Forest really fast!

START

FINISH

Can you help us find the path to the Swinging Forest?

We made it!

Le**ó**n knows a trick that can take us through
the Swinging Forest really fast!
Connect the dots to find out what his trick is.

Will you draw a swing for me to swing on?

We have to watch out for Swiper!
He'll try to swipe León's circus toys.

Do you see Swiper?

Oh, no!

León can't be in the Circus without his circus toys.
We have to find them!

Do you see León's circus ball and Hula-Hoop?

Find the path that goes to Tightrope Bridge.

Find 3 things that are different in the bottom picture!

We made it across Tightrope Bridge!

Do you see the circus tent?

We need something to help get us to the Circus FAST!
Will you check Backpack and circle something we can use?

How many pairs of roller skates do we need?

Draw a line from the skate to the matching helmet.

Let's get to the Circus so León can become a circus lion!

We made it! Let's decorate the circus flags.

Draw León's tightrope.

The ringmaster wants León to join the Circus!

We did it!

Bouncy Ball

Boots and I are at the toy store. Boots is going to buy a new bouncy ball! Do you see a ball?

The ball costs 12 coins.
I bet I have some coins in Backpack.

Can you find 12 coins?

Boots loves his bouncy ball!

Do you see 6 things that are round like the bouncy ball?

Wait! Wait! The ball is bouncing away!

Will you check Map
to find out where the ball is going?

We'll have to cross the Mucky Mud, then go over
Troll Bridge. And that's how we'll get to
the Volcano to get Boots's ball!

START

FINISH

To get through the Mucky Mud,
we have to follow the numbers from 1 to 10.

Trace the path that will take us to Troll Bridge.

We're at Troll Bridge! Do you see the Grumpy Old Troll?

The Troll won't let us over his bridge unless we can solve his riddle. Bouncy, bouncy, bouncy, bounce. Will you circle the 2 things that bounce?

**Yay! We made it over Troll Bridge.
Where do we go next?**

Tico said he'll help us get to the Volcano fast!
But his car is missing some pieces.
Can you find the door, the tire, and the steering wheel?

Oh, no! Swiper swiped Boots's bouncy ball!

Swiper is throwing the ball into the Volcano!

The Volcano is erupting! Do you see the ball?

KABOOM! The Volcano is raining bouncy balls. Yay!

Boots and bouncy ball both begin with the letter B.
Find 2 more things that begin with the letter B.

It's Fiesta Time!

Hi, I'm Dora! Boots and I love being silly!

Silly Mail Bird has brought us an invitation.

Big Red Chicken is having a Super Silly Fiesta.
There's nothing super sillier than a Super Silly Fiesta!

Draw a silly, squiggly line to match each party hat to a balloon.

I hear Big Red Chicken. He can't find his cake
for the party. C'mon, we can help him!

We'll go through the Singing Gate and over the Troll Bridge to get to the Super Silly Fiesta.

What is making all that noise?

Dora's cousin, Diego, knows something is wrong.
These silly animals have mixed up their sounds.

Will you help Diego match each animal to its sound?

RIBBIT

MOO

WOOF

QUACK

We figured out all the animals' sounds.

Trace the path that leads to the Singing Gate.

Benny is practicing his juggling for the Super Silly Fiesta.

Do you see Swiper?
He is going to swipe Benny's juggling balls.

**Swiper hid Benny's juggling balls.
Can you help Benny find all 7 of them?**

Thanks for finding my juggling balls.

To get over the bridge, Dora and Boots have to
make the Grumpy Old Troll laugh.
Help them by drawing silly things on the page!

You made the Grumpy Old Troll laugh!
Now Dora and Boots can go over the bridge.

Look, there's the Super Silly Fiesta at the top of the hill!

Tico can help fly us to the top of the hill.

Help us catch the stars by coloring them!

Draw a silly line from each star to the Star Pocket on Backpack!

We made it to the Super Silly Fiesta!
Let's help Big Red Chicken find his cake.

Do you see Big Red Chicken's cake?

**Right! The cake is on Big Red Chicken's head.
That's so silly!**

Now that we've found my cake,
we can have the Super Silly Fiesta!

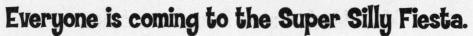
Everyone is coming to the Super Silly Fiesta.

Flap your arms and do the Silly Chicken Dance!

Funny Star and his star friends can help make
the Super Silly Fiesta really super silly.
To call the stars out of the Star Pocket, say *estrellas!*

Monster Bash!

Boo! It's me, Dora. I'm wearing my cat costume for Halloween.

Happy Halloween, Boots! What's your costume?

I'm a fire chicken! I couldn't decide between a chicken and a firefighter. So I'm both! *Bawk! Bawk!*

Whooaa! You surprised us, Little Monster!

Dora, when the little arrow on the Big Clock
gets to the 12, all monsters must be home! But I'm lost.

What time is it now? Help Little Monster find out by looking at the number that the little hand is pointing to. Then draw that many circles below the clock.

The clock says it's 9! We'd better check Map to find out how to get to Little Monster's house.

Map says we have to go through the Pumpkin Patch and the Good Witch's Forest to get to Little Monster's house.

Will you help us find the Pumpkin Patch?
Trace the path that leads to it.

Look at all the silly bats! How many do you see?

Help Dora's friends find their Halloween costumes by following the lines!

Hey! We can trick-or-treat on the way to Little Monster's house.

Treats! Hooray! Thank you! ¡Gracias!

There's our friend Scarecrow in the Pumpkin Patch.
He can help us get Little Monster home.

**To get through the Patch, the scarecrow says
find the pumpkins that match.**

Will you help me find the jack-o'-lantern that matches mine?

I hear the Big Clock! Will you help us find out what time it is? First count the pieces of candy in my goody bag. Then draw an arrow to that number on the Big Clock.

Now we have to find the Good Witch's Forest. But look! It's Abuela's house. Can you guess what her costume will be? Connect the dots for a hint.

I see more trick-or-treaters! What is Diego dressed as?
What is Big Red Chicken dressed as?

Did you hear that? That sounds like Swiper! That sneaky fox will try to swipe our candy. Do you see Swiper?

Swiper, no swiping!

Swiper, if you want some candy, just say, "Trick or treat!"

It's the Big Clock! Help Dora and Little Monster find out what time it is by following the path with the triangles.

We made it! The Good Witch's Forest is on the other side of the gate! To open the gate, say, "Abre."

The Good Witch is giving us her broomstick so we can fly quickly through the Forest.

We have to fly through the Forest toward the moon! Will you help us fly toward the moon?

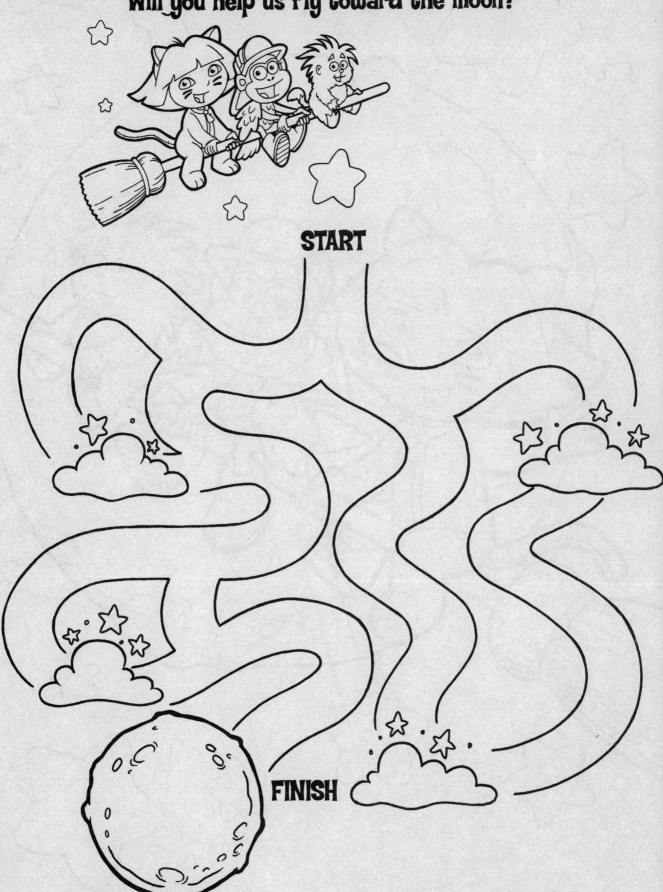

START

FINISH

Whooo-hooo! Wheeee!

Yay, look! *¡Estrellas!* Help us catch the stars by using the chart to color them.

1=Yellow
2=Blue
3=Red
4=Orange
5=Green

We're almost to Little Monster's house! But we'd better hurry. Which path will get us there the quickest?

It's 12 o'clock! We brought Little Monster home just in time for . . . the Halloween Party! And we're invited, too!

We did it! Thanks for helping! Happy Halloween!